A bus came to the school.
The children climbed in.
'I like going out,' said Wilf.
'Don't push,' said Mrs May.

The bus set off.
'Hooray!' shouted the children.
'We're going to the zoo.'
'Don't shout, children,' said Mrs May.

Biff sat with Chip.
Wilf sat with Nadim.
'This is fun,' shouted Nadim.
'It is if you don't shout,' said Mrs May.

The bus stopped on the way.
The children climbed out.
Some children looked at the water.
Some children went to the toilet.

'Don't run away,' said Mrs May, 'and
don't go too near the water.'

Wilf kicked a stone and his shoe came off.
The shoe landed in the water with
  a splash.
'Oh Wilf!' said Biff.

Wilf couldn't get his shoe.
He told Mrs May about it.
'What a silly thing to do!' she said.
'I don't know what we can do.'

When they got to the zoo it began to
   rain.
The children climbed out of the bus and
   Mrs May went to get the tickets.

Nadim wanted to see the elephants.
Wilf wanted to see the lions and
    Biff wanted to see the crocodiles.
'I hope the rain stops,' said Mrs May.

It rained and rained.
The children were fed up.
The animals were fed up too.
'Don't get wet,' said Mrs May.

The rain didn't stop so the children
climbed back on the bus.
'Can we go to the museum?' asked Nadim.
'What a good idea!' said Mrs May.

They went to a museum.
'This is good,' said Wilf.
'We can see dinosaurs here.'
'I like dinosaurs,' said Nadim.

They began to run towards the dinosaurs.
'Don't run,' called Mrs May.
'The dinosaurs won't go away.'

They looked at a big dinosaur.
'What is this one called?' asked Wilf.
'I don't know yet,' said Nadim.
'Let's go and see.'

Biff had her camera.
She took a photograph of the dinosaur.
'What is it called?' she asked.
'It's an apatosaurus,' said Nadim.

The children went into a room.
A lady told them about dinosaurs and
    showed them some pictures.

'I know what that one
   is called,' said Nadim.
'It's called an apatosaurus.'
'Good, Nadim,' said Mrs May.

The children went to the shop.
Wilf got a book about dinosaurs.
Nadim got a model to make.
It was a model of an apatosaurus.

'I can make it at home,' he said.
Chip said, 'Come to our house.
We can help you.'

The bus got back to school.
It was time to go home.
'Thank you,' said the children.
'Thank you for a lovely day.'

'Goodbye, Mrs May,' said Nadim.
'Can we draw dinosaurs tomorrow?'
'What a good idea!' said Mrs May.

Nadim and Wilf went home with
   Biff and Chip.
They went to Chip's room and
   began to make the model.

The magic key began to glow.
Biff ran to the box and picked it up.
'Come on,' she called. 'It's time for
a magic adventure.'

'Come on Nadim,' called Chip.
'We're going on a magic adventure.
We're going to the land of
    the dinosaurs.'

Printed in Hong Kong